One Day There Was Nothing to Do

Written by Jill Creighton
Art by Ruth Ohi

Annick Press, Toronto, Canada

Second Printing, March 1991

Annick Press

Annick Press gratefully acknowledges the
support of The Canada Council and the Ontario
Arts Council

Canadian Cataloguing in Publication Data

Creighton, Jill
   One day there was nothing to do

ISBN 1-55037-091-X (bound).—ISBN 1-55037-090-1 (pbk.)

I. Ohi, Ruth.   II. Title.

PS 8555.R44305 1990   jC813′.54   C89-095299-X
PZ7.C74On 1990

Distribution in Canada and the USA:
Firefly Books Ltd.
250 Sparks Avenue
Willowdale, Ontario
M2H 2S4

∞ Printed on acid free paper

Printed and bound in Canada
by Friesen Printers, Altona, Manitoba

For Rob

One day there was nothing to do. So we went to tell Ma.
"I guess you'll have to think of something," she said.

We thought, . . . and thought, . . . and thought, . . . and then . . . a giant ferocious snapping turtle got into the back hall.

We went to tell Ma.

"Oh, no," she said. We thought she'd be afraid.

But she went to the kitchen cupboard to get some pie tins to bang together to scare the turtle.

"Stay back, boys," she said. "Stay back, Rosalie. Don't be afraid. We'll deal with this."

She leaped into the back hall smacking her pie tins together.

"Get out," she yelled in a fearsome voice. But the ferocious snapping turtle had already gone. Ma yelled out the back door after it: "You stay away."

Then she came back in.

"There, children," she said, "we're quite safe."

"Thank you, Ma," we said.

At snack time a furry
nibbling mouse gobbled up all
our crackers and cheese and
left crumbs all over the floor.
We went to tell Ma.

"How dreadful. What a nerve." said Ma. "That's outrageous. You will have to help me deal with this. You know I worry about mice."

Ma climbed up on the counter. We poked under the fridge and stove with a broom handle.

"There he goes," we yelled.

"Where?" yelled Ma.

"He jumped out the window."

"Thank heavens," said Ma. She climbed down off the counter.

"Get the dustpan, Harry," she said, "and all of you clean up. I'll get you another plate of cheese and crackers, you poor things."

"Thank you, Ma," we said.

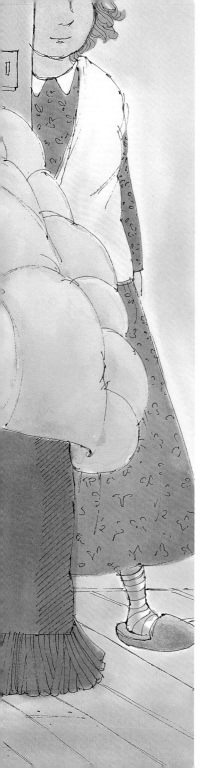

In the afternoon, when we were playing upstairs, wild pigs got under Rosalie's bed.

We called for Ma and pretty soon she came running up.

"Wild pigs are under my bed," yelled Rosalie.

Ma screamed and jumped onto a chair.

"We saw their curling little tails," we told her,
"and we heard them snuffling. They plan to eat
our slippers."
  "Not the new furry bunny slippers," said Ma.
  We nodded.
  "Oh no," said Ma. "Get back, Pete. I'll scare
them out with this trumpet."

One pig ran out but there were still two more.
"They're not afraid of trumpets," we told Ma.
"Oh, dear," she said, "that's bothersome. We'll
have to use a drum and stamp our feet."

So Ma leaned down and banged on the drum and we stamped our feet as hard as we could.

That did it. The pigs clattered down the stairs and out the front door.

Ma didn't see them.

"Well, that's a shame," she said. "I wanted to see their curling tails. You'd better check to see if your slippers are safe."

There was only a little wet bit on one bunny ear. Ma hung the slipper on the line to dry.

 At bath time the most dreadful thing of all happened. A poisonous snake joined us in the bath.
Ma was horrified.
"Get out," she yelled at us.
"But we're not washed yet!"
"Oh, dear," she said, "you have to wash. Wait, I have an idea."
She ran into the kitchen and came back with a big sieve.
"Get back," she said, "I'll capture it in this."
She chased the snake around the bath water with the sieve but it always slithered out at the last minute.

Then she put on her rubber gloves and tried to catch it with her hands. It was no use.

Next she got a sponge and tried to knock it into a bucket. That didn't work and Ma got wet.

"Kids," she said, "I'm afraid you'll have to get out of the bath without washing."

"That's a shame," said Rosalie, and pulled the plug. The snake got sucked down with the bath water. Ma thought she saw the tip of its tail go down.

"What an exciting day," she said. "I'm quite exhausted."

She read us a story and tucked us into bed.

"Good night. Sweet dreams."

The End